Mule
School

For Ben and Tom, with love
J.R.

To Shane
L.C.

Text © Julia Rawlinson 2007 • Illustrations © Lynne Chapman 2007

Original edition published in Great Britain in 2007 by Gullane Children's Books, an imprint of Pinwheel Limited,
Winchester House, 259-269 Old Marylebone Road, London, NW1 5XJ, England.

Printed and bound in China

Library of Congress Cataloging-in-Publication Data available.

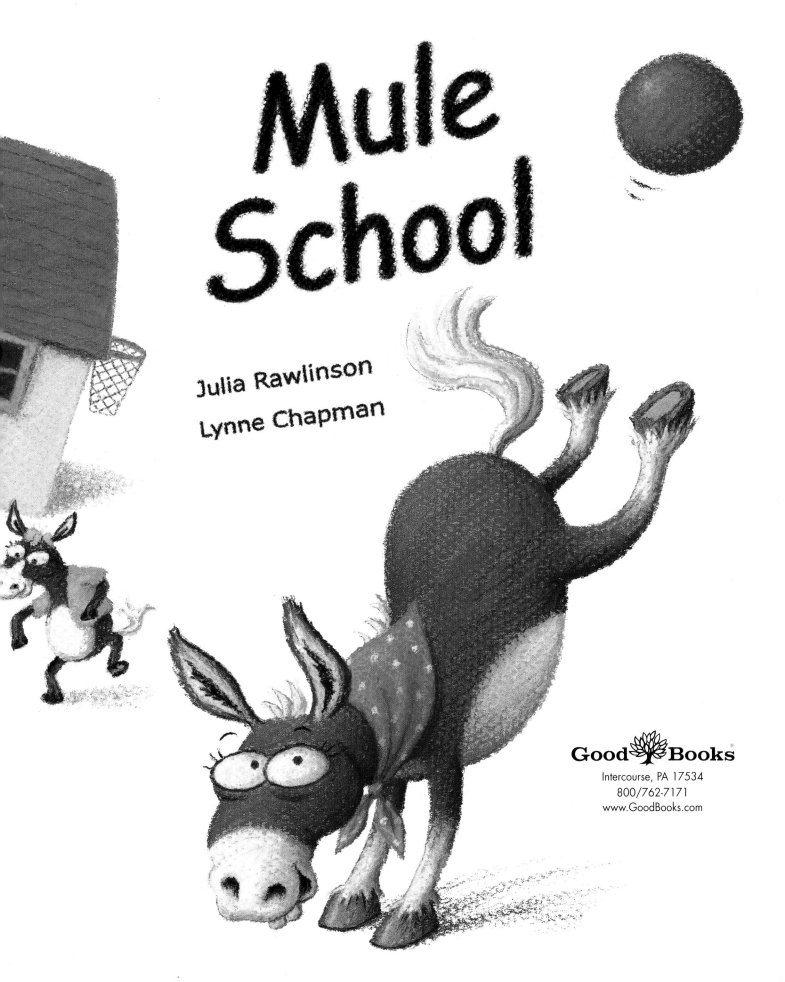

Mule
School

Julia Rawlinson

Lynne Chapman

Good Books

Intercourse, PA 17534
800/762-7171
www.GoodBooks.com

Stomper did not like **Mule School**. He liked the other mules. He liked lunchtime and playtime. But he did not like *Stubbornness Practice*.

How we say
"NO"

"NOT A CHANCE"

"GO AWAY"

"NEVER"

"WON'T"

BASH Class 2

BIFF Class 2

BIM-BAM Class 2

STOMPER Class 2

Every day his schedule was the same:

9 o'clock: **Stubbornness**

11 o'clock: **Kicking**

12 o'clock: **Lunch**

1 o'clock: **Stubbornness**

3 o'clock: **Kicking**

4 o'clock: **Home**

Day after day the mules recited
"Won't, won't, won't" and "Never, never, never."
They **SHOOK** their heads and **STAMPED** their feet.

But one day Stomper put his hoof in the air. "What if we *want* to do as we're told?" he asked nervously.

"You are a mule. Refuse!" cried Mrs. Kick.

"But what if it seems like a good idea?" mumbled Stomper.
"Nobody else's idea is good," she snapped, and sent him to stand in the corner.

Stomper's first **stubbornness test** was to guard a pile of apples. He stood mumbling "*No, no, no*" under his breath, but before long a scruffy pig snuffled up.

"My piglets are hungry. Could you spare some apples?" she asked. "Of course," nodded Stomper. "Help yourself."

The pig waddled happily off with
the apples, but then Stomper gulped.
He had forgotten to be stubborn.

"Fool of a mule," cried Mrs. Kick.
"You must never, ever
give in to a pig."

Stomper's next task
was to block a path.

Soon a family of goats needed to
get past. Stomper stood aside and
waved them by politely . . .

But then the school's
meanest mules, Biff and Bash,
jumped out and laughed.
*"We are mules, we like to kick.
Weakness makes us
sick, sick, sick!"*
they chanted as they circled him.

"We're going to tell on you.
You were meant to stop the
goats, not let them through."

"They're right," thought Stomper sadly. "I am a useless mule."

"Stamper, why am I so weak?"
asked Stomper on the playground.
"You're not weak. You've got a good kick,"
said Stamper. "Come and play bash ball."

He walloped the ball over the
straw store and Stomper galloped after it,
forgetting all his troubles as he raced across
the yard. They bashed and butted, kicked
and crashed until it was time for class.

That afternoon there was a field trip to practice kicking in the valley, but Stomper was sent out apple-picking to replace the apples he had lost.

He wandered up the valley,
following a butterfly. As he listened
to the mules chanting below,
he heard another sound.

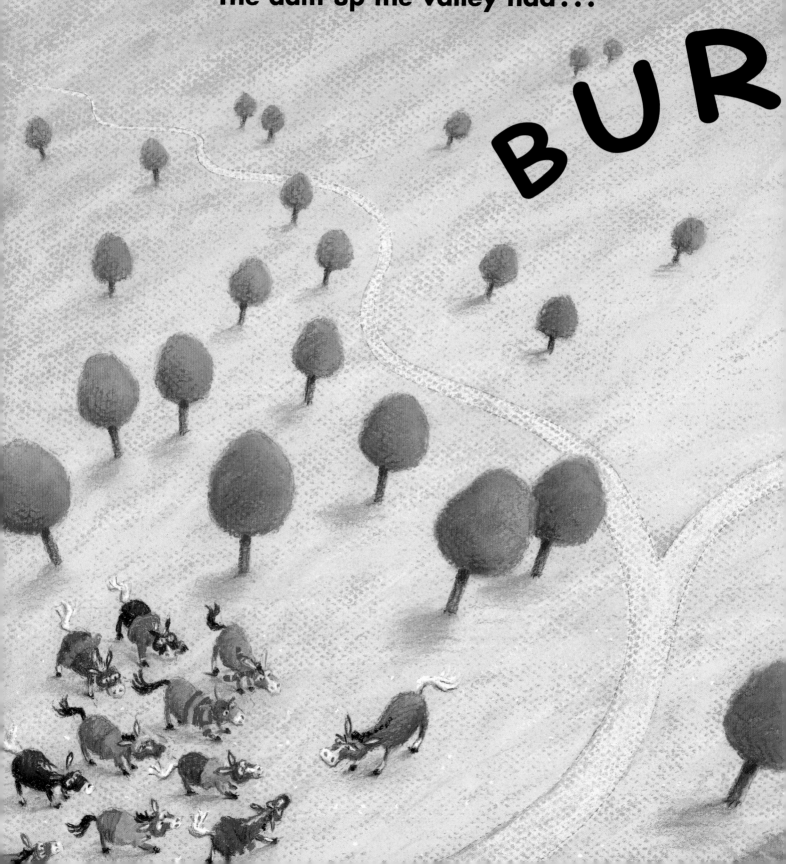

The dam up the valley had . . .

BUR

ST!

And a great river was roaring down. His friends were going to be . . .

swept away!

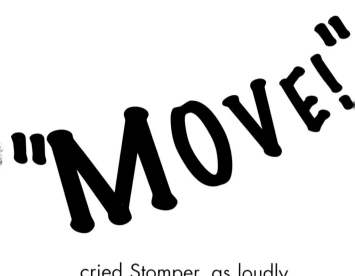

cried Stomper, as loudly
as he could, but the mules
didn't hear him.

"Leaf or branch
or rock or stick,
whatever it is
we'll give it a . . .

kick!"

they chanted,
far below.

"RUN!"

thundered Stomper, waving
his hooves wildly, but
the mules were not looking.

"Nose to the ground
and tail to the sky,
let those thundering
mule hooves . . .

fly!"

they cried as they
kick-kick-kicked.

Then, at last, Mrs. Kick saw the water swooshing towards her. She faced up the valley, dug in her hooves, bared her teeth and cried,

"We are mules and we won't budge, even for an . . .

ENORMOUS FLOOD!"

The other mules took
up the cry. Their eyes
were wide, their ears were
back, but their trembling
hooves were planted
firmly in the mud.

Suddenly another sound rose above the rushing water.

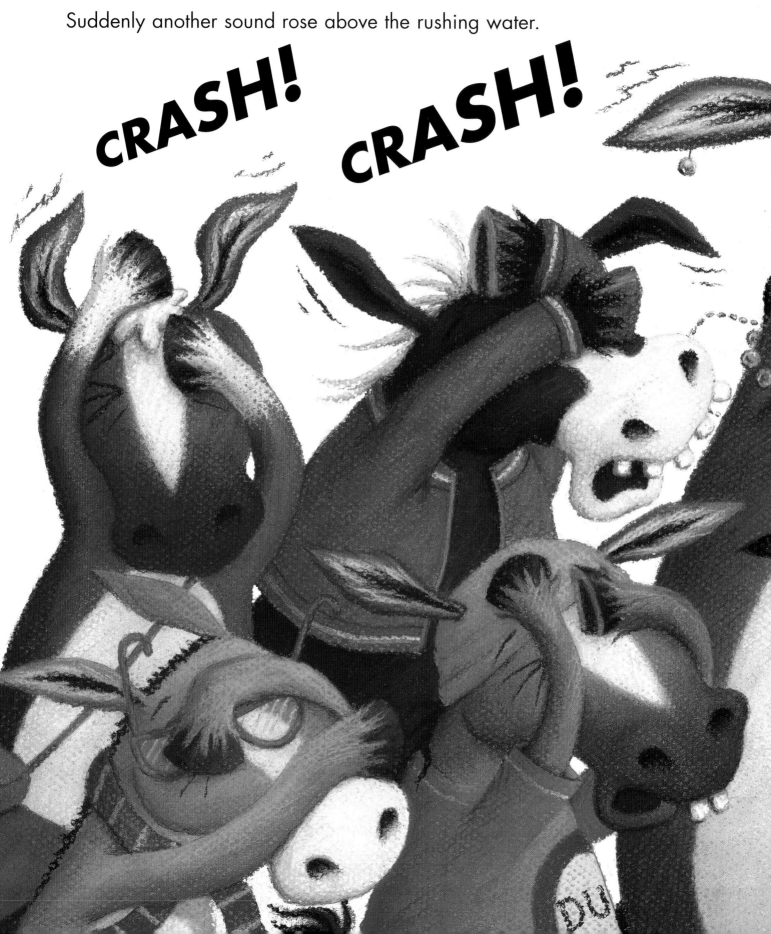

CRASH!

The mules screwed their eyes tight shut and covered their heads with their hooves, but then . . .

"IT'S STOMPER!"

cried Stamper with a mighty neigh of delight. Stomper's head was down, his heels were flying and he was **kick-kick-kicking** with all his might.

CRA

CRASH!

CRASH!

CRA

SH!

H!

He kicked at rocks; he kicked at
sticks; he kicked at broken branches.
Wood and rock tumbled down
the valley with a rumbling roar,
making a new dam that whooshed
the water safely away.

Stomper trotted down the hill and stood, casually
nibbling flowers. Slowly the other mules sidled up.
"We were wrong," they muttered. "We were foolish mules."

Stomper shook his head.
"No," he said, "you stood your
ground. You did what a mule should
do. It's just good that not all mules
are exactly the same."

Mrs. Kick looked thoughtful as
she led them back to school.

Next day at Mule School the schedule read:

9 o'clock: **Stubbornness or Pottery**

11 o'clock: **Kicking or Flower Arranging**

12 o'clock: Lunch

1 o'clock: **Stubbornness or Hoof Printing**

3 o'clock: **Kicking or Musical Mules**

4 o'clock: Home

101 Refusals
KICKING: high
KICKING: low
Flowers are FUN!
POTTERY for beginners
NO WAY JOSÉ!
Mule Tunes
Animal Arts & Crafts
Just Say "No"!

And at 11 o'clock, while Stomper happily kicked his way through class . . .

...Biff and Bash were down in the meadow, merrily arranging daisies.